George B. Sowerby

Appendix to Marine Shells of South Africa

a catalogue of all the known species - with references to figures in various

works, descriptions of new species

George B. Sowerby

Appendix to Marine Shells of South Africa
*a catalogue of all the known species - with references to figures in various works,
descriptions of new species*

ISBN/EAN: 9783337392109

Printed in Europe, USA, Canada, Australia, Japan

Cover: Foto ©Andreas Hilbeck / pixelio.de

More available books at **www.hansebooks.com**

APPENDIX TO

MARINE SHELLS

OF

SOUTH AFRICA

A CATALOGUE OF ALL THE KNOWN SPECIES

WITH

REFERENCES TO FIGURES IN VARIOUS WORKS, DESCRIPTIONS
OF NEW SPECIES, AND FIGURES OF SUCH AS ARE NEW,
LITTLE KNOWN, OR HITHERTO UNFIGURED.

BY

G. B. SOWERBY, F.L.S., F.Z.S.

LONDON:
SOWERBY, 121, FULHAM ROAD, S.W.
1897.

PREFACE.

SINCE the publication of "Marine Shells of South Africa" in 1892, a considerable number of additional species has been discovered, some well known as inhabiting other seas, and others new to science. Descriptions without figures of some of these were published in the "Journal of Conchology," 1894. The time has now come for the publication, in the form of an appendix to the original work, of descriptions of the new species, with figures of those hitherto unfigured, together with a list (as complete as possible) of all the species found up to date in South African Waters, and not included in my work of 1892, giving references to figures in well-known works. I include a list of emendations referring to the pages of the 1st Volume, altering some of the generic names in accordance with the nomenclature now in use. These changes are somewhat inconvenient, but they are rendered necessary by the law of priority. The number of additional South African Marine Mollusca enumerated in the present work is 311, bringing up the grand total to 1051. The greater number of these have come under my observation, but some are quoted on the authority of Krauss, Gould, and other authors, and are unknown to me. The three plates in the present work following the five originally published, and numbered accordingly, vi., vii., viii., give 74 figures of 56 species.

Again I have pleasure in tendering my grateful acknowledgments to friends resident in South Africa, after whom I have named some of the species, and particularly to John H. Ponsonby, Esq., for the material which has enabled me to make this contribution to South African Conchology.

G. B. SOWERBY.

MARINE SHELLS

OF

SOUTH AFRICA.

--

ADDITIONAL SPECIES.

-

GASTROPODA.

MUREX RAMOSUS, *Linn.*, Sowerby, Thes. Conch., vol. iv., pl. 387, fig. 69.—Natal Common in the Indian Ocean.

MUREX TRIVIALIS, *A. Adams*, Sow. Thes. Conch., vol. iv., pl. 388, fig. 80.—Natal.

FULGUR AFRICANUS. *Sowerby*, nov. sp. (pl. 6, fig. 19.) Testa elongato-pyriformis, albida, fusco suffusa, flammis conspicuis fuscis longitudinaliter picta ; spira breviter conica, gradata; apice ? (fracto); anfractus spiraliter confertim sulcati, angulati, ad angulum nodulis parum elevatis muniti ; anfractus ultimus supra angulum planato declivis, infra convexiusculus, in cauda longiuscula desinens, ubique densissime longitudinaliter striatus, spiraliter liratus, liris numerosis, lævigatis, parum elevatis; apertura oblongo-ovata ; canalis longus, mediocriter latus, rectus; columella leviter incurvata ; labrum tenue.

Long. 32, diam. 16 millim.

Hab. Port Elizabeth.

Although this may be a young shell, it is certainly distinct from the dextral form of *F. berversus*.

The longitudinal flames are rather broad, distant and irregularly waved on the back of the shell, not (as in *F. carica*) marking the periods of growth.

I have only seen two specimens of this species, both collected at Port Elizabeth. They are about equal in size.

FUSUS CRENULATUS, Sowerby, Thes. Conch., vol iv., p. 85, pl. 14, fig. 170.—Cape of Good Hope.

Tryon opines that this is a *Siphonalia*, but in the absence of evidence, I think it best for the present to place it with *Fusus*.

EUTHRIA MAGELLANI, *Vélain*, Arch. Zool. Exper. et Gen. 1877, vol. vi., p. 104, pl. 2, figs. 8-11.—Natal. The type is from St. Paul's Island.

PISANIA TRITONOIDES, *Reeve.* (*Buccinum*), Conch. Icon. sp. 77.—Cape of Good Hope (Gould). Durban.

METULA CLATHRATA, *Adams and Reeve*, Voy. Samarang, p. 32, pl. 11, fig. 12.—Cape of Good Hope, 136 fathoms.

PLEUROTOMA TIGRINA, *Lamarck*, Reeve, Conch. Icon. (*Pleurotoma*) fig. 3.—Durban. Common in many localities from Mauritius to the Philippines and South Sea Islands.

PLEUROTOMA CINGULIFERA, *Lamarck*, Reeve, Conch. Icon. fig. 1.—Durban. Distribution about the same as the last.

PLEUROTOMA MONILIFERA, *Pease*, Proc. Zool. Soc. 1860, p. 398. Tryon, Man. of Conch. vol. vi , p. 173, pl. 4, fig. 52 (as var. of *P. gemmata*, Hinds).

PLEUROTOMA (DRILLIA) LAVARDI, *Sowerby*, n. sp. pl. 8, fig. 3, 4. Testa turrita, rufo-fusca, lævigata, longitudinaliter costata ; anfractus 7 obtusissime angulati, supra angulum leviter concavi, infra convexiusculi, costis circ. 11 rotundatis lævibus, obliquiusculis instructi ; ultimus spiram fere æquans ad basin leviter alternatus haud rostratus, spiraliter tenuisulcatus ; apertura ob'ongo-ovata ; columella rectiuscula superne valde callosa ; labrum arcuatum, sinu latiusculo, haud profundo emarginatum.

Long 11, diam 4 millim.

Hab. Pondoland. Port Elizabeth.

This species has long been mistaken for *P. castanea* Reeve, but upon comparison with the type of that species it is found to be quite distinct.

PLEUROTOMA (DRILLIA) BURNUPI, *Sowerby*, n. sp.   (Plate 8, fig. 1, 2.)

Testa turrita, rufo-fusca, fascia albida interrupta et linea fusca ornata; spira acuta; anfractus 8, obtuse angulati, superne declives, costis circ. 10 lævibus parum elevatis leviter obliquis instructi ; ultimus spiram vix æquans, leviter intortus, inferne lævigatus, ad basim liratus, haud rostratus ; apertura latiuscula, intus dilute fusca ; columella suboblique arcuata, superne tubercula parviuscula instructa ; labrum tenue, sinu postico latiusculo.

Long. 10, diam. 4 millim.

Hab. Durban.

Allied to *P. Layardi*, with a sharper spire; the somewhat oblique and distant ribs run to the top of the whorls, and become obsolete on the lower half of the body whorl.   The reddish brown colour of the shell is relieved by an interrupted whitish band at the angle, surmounted by a thin dark brown line.

CLATHURELLA VERRUCOSA, *Sowerby*, nov. sp. (pl. 6, fig. 14).   Testa parva, breviter ovata, rugosa, fusca, spira conica, gradata ; anfractus 5, primi 2 læves, sequentes biangulati, liris spiralibus 2, crassis confertis valde nodulosis instructi ; sutura late canaliculata ; anfractus ultimus spiram superans, superne angulatus. basin versus leviter attenuatus, haud rostratus, undique nodulosus ; apertura latiuscula ; labrum vix incrassatum ; sinu postico latiusculo.

Long. 2.75., diam. 1.50 millim.

Hab Port Elizabeth.

This species was erroneously referred by me on page 7 of "Marine Shells of South Africa," as *Mangelia clathrata*, M. de Serres, from which upon further examination I find it to be quite distinct.

CLATHURELLA COMMODA, *Smith*, Ann. and Mag. of Nat. Hist., 1882.—South Africa (Smith).

MANGILIA CEREA, *Carpenter*, Ann. and Mag. of Nat. Hist., 1865, p 400.—Cape Town.

MANGILIA CASTA, *Reeve*, Conch. Icon. (Mang.), pl. 7, f. 55.— Kalk Bay. Tryon (vol. vi., p. 305) proposed the name of *Daphnella Reeveana* for this species, on account of the pre-occupation of the name by Hinds in the genus *Pleurotoma*, and considering both to be *Daphnella*. It seems to me, how-ever, that Reeve's species is a true *Mangilia*, while that of Hinds is, though somewhat uncertain, probably a *Daphnella*, certainly not a *Mangilia*.

ᵛ   LOTORIUM GEMMATUM, *Reeve*, Conch. Icon. (*Triton*), sp. 60.—
Natal.   This species is common in many localities from
Mauritius to the South Pacific Islands.

ᵧ   LOTORIUM (PRIENE) MURRAYI, *Smith* (*Lampusia*), Proc.
Zool. Soc. 1891, p. 436, pl. 34, fig. 1.—Off Cape of Good
Hope in 150 fathoms (Voy. of Challenger).

ᐟ   LOTORIUM GALLINAGO, *Reeve*, Conch. Icon. (*Triton*), pl. 1,
fig. 3.—Durban.

        LOTORIUM CHLOROSTOMA, *Lamarck*, Reeve, Conch. Icon.
(*Triton*), fig. 3.—Durban.   W dely distributed in the Indian
Ocean, etc.

        LOTORIUM MONILIFERRUM, *Adams and Reeve*, Voy. of
Samarang Moll., pl. 10, fig. 18.—Durban.

ᐟ   LOTORIUM TUBEROSUM, *Lamarck*, Reeve, Conch. Icon.
(*Triton*), fig. 1.—Durban.   Widely distributed in the Indian
and Pacific Oceans.

        ·LOTORIUM CYNOCEPHALUM, *Lamarck*, Reeve, Conch. Icon.
(*Triton*), fig. 26 –-Durban ; also Mauritius, Ceylon, Philippines, etc.

        LOTORIUM GRACILE, *Reeve*, Conch. Icon. (*Triton*), fig. 58.—
Durban.

        LOTORIUM ELONGATUM, *Reeve*, Conch. Icon. (*Triton*),
sp. 59.—Durban.

        LOTORIUM PYRUM, *Reeve*, Conch. Icon. (*Triton*), sp. 33.—
Durban.

        LOTORIUM ENCAUSTICUM, *Reeve*, Conch. Icon. (*Triton*),
sp. 43.—Durban.

        LOTORIUM (LAGENA) CINGULATUM, *Pfeiffer*, Reeve, Conch.
Icon. (*Triton*), fig. 35.—Durban.

        LOTORIUM (PERSONA) ANUS, *Lamarck*, Reeve, Conch. Icon.
(*Triton*), fig. 44.—Natal.   This species is pretty common at
Mauritius.

        RANELLA AFFINIS, *Broderip*, Reeve, Conch. Icon. (*Ranella*),
fig. 19.—Durban.   I have some doubt whether this is more
than a variety of *R. granifera*, Lam.

        COMINELLA UNIFASCIATA, VAR. CONCOLOR, *Sowerby*, var.
nov. In form the same as type, but of a uniform reddish brown
colour, without band.—Natal.

BULLIA PUSTULOSA. *Sowerby* (plate 6, fig. 1). Journal of Conchology, April 1894, p. 5.—Durban.

BULLIA CAPENSIS, *Euthyme*, Bull. de la Soc. Malac. de France, vol. ii. p. 237.—Port Elizabeth. Unfigured, and unknown to me. May be a form of *B. digitalis.*

BULLIA SIMILIS, *Sowerby*, nov. sp. (pl. 7, fig 1.) Testa acuminata, solidiuscula, albida, lineis numerosis stramineis undulatis longitudinis picta ; spira acuta ; anfractus 8. convexiusculi, undique spiraliter sulcati, superne liris granulosis instructi ; sutura anguste canaliculata, lira pustulata marginata ; anfractus ultimus spiram fere æquans, ad basin profunde canaliculatus ; columella leviter contorta, tenuiter callosa, extus acute lirata ; apertura ovata, fauce dilute fusca.

Long. 31, diam. maj. 15 millim.

Hab. Natal.

This species is very like *B. Belangeri*, Kiener, in form and colouring, but distinguished by the distinctly granular ridges on the upper part of the whorls. It may, possibly, be only a variety, but I have examined more than a hundred specimens of *B. Belangeri* without finding the slightest trace of these characteristic bead-like granules on any.

NASSA ALGIDA, *Reeve*, Conch. Icon. (*Nassa*), fig. 145.—Natal.

NASSA PICTA, *Dunker*, Reeve, Conch. Icon. (*Nassa*), pl. 2, fig. 9.—Natal (Gibbons.)

NASSA COCCINELLA, *Lamarck*, An. Sans. Vert., vii., p. 274.—Algoa Bay (Gibbons). This is probably the *N. coccinea*, A. Adams. I doubt its identity with *N. incrassata.*

NASSA RUFULA, *Kiener* (*Buccinum*), Reeve, Conch. Icon. (*Nassa*), pl. 2, fig. 14.—Natal. Known as an Australian species.

NASSA HORRIDA, *Dunker* (*Buccinum*), Reeve, Conch. Icon. pl. 11, fig. 69.—Natal.

NASSA FENESTRATA, *Marrat*, "New Forms of Nassa" 1887, p. 10 ; Tr. on, Man. of Conch., vol. iv., p. 57, pl. 16, fig. 280, as var. of *N. albescens.*—Natal (Gibbons).

NASSA SIGNATA, *Dunker*, Tryon, Man. of Conch., vol. iv., p. 57, pl. 17, fig. 327—South Africa (Tryon).

NASSA KOCHIANA, *Dunker*, Tryon, Man. of Conch , vol. iv., pl. 17, fig. 334.—Cape (Krauss), Table Bay (Tryon).

NASSA PRODUCTA, Sowerby, n. sp. (plate 8, fig. 4, 5.) Testa elongato-turrita, pallide lutescens, fusco unifasciata, spira perclata, leviter convexa, ad apicem acuta; anfractus 9, rotunde convexi, sutura impressa sejuncti, costis longitudinis numerosis crassis instructi, spiraliter tenuiter lirati; ultimus brevis, rotundatus, ad basin excavatus; apertura rotunde ovata, intus lirata; labrum tenue, extus varicosum; columella rugosa.

Long. 13.50, diam. 5 millim.
Hab. Durban.
A shell allied to *N. incrassata*, but of a very elongated form.

NASSARIA ACUMINATA, *Reeve*, Conch. Icon. (*Triton*), pl. 14, fig. 54.—Durban.

PURPURA DUBIA, *Krauss*, is COMINELLA LAGENARIA.

PURPURA CASTANEA, *Krauss*, Küster Monog. p. 170, pl. 28, figs. 8, 9.—Cape of Good Hope (Krauss).

PURPURA (IOPAS) SITULA, *Reeve*, Conch. Icon. (*Buccinum*) pl. 6, fig. 40.—Durban (Turton).

SISTRUM UNDATUM, *Chemnitz*, Tryon, Man. of Conch. vol. ii., p. 189, pl 59, fig. 259 and 261. *Murex margariticola*, Brod., Reeve, Conch. Icon (*Murex*), fig. 178.—Durban. Delagoa Bay (Gibbons).

SISTRUM ELONGATUM, *Blainville*, Reeve, Conch. Icon. (*Ricinula*), pl. 4, fig. 25.—Durban.

SISTRUM MUTICUM, *Lamk*, Reeve, Conch. Icon. (*Ricinula*), pl. 2, fig. 6.—Durban.

SISTRUM AFFINE, *Peas*, Proc. Zool. Soc. 1862. Tryon vol. ii., pl. 57, fig. 228, as var. of *S. Marginatrum*.

SISTRUM PARVULUM, *Gould*, Proc. Bost. Soc. vii., p. 328. Simon's Bay (Stimpson). Probably a var. of *S. Marginatrum*.

SISTRUM CONCATENATUM, *Lamarck*, Reeve, Conch. Icon. (*Ricinula*), sp. 18.—Durban.

SISTRUM CORONATUM, *H. Adams*, Proc, Zool Soc. 1869, p. 272, pl. 19, fig. 4.—Natal. A specimen much larger than those from Mauritius.

CORALLIOPHILA FRITSCHI, *Martens*, Jahrb. Mal. Gesell. i., p. 135, pl. 6, fig. 3. Tryon vol. ii., p. 208, pl. 65, fig. 352. —False Bay (Martens).

OLIVA TRUNCATA, *Marrat*, Sowerby, Thes Conch., vol. iv., pl. 331, fig. 41.—Cape of Good Hope (*Marrat*).

OLIVA MICANS, *Solander*, Sowerby, Thes. Conch., vol. iv., pl. 345. figs 294-296. *O. nana*, Lam.—S Africa (Tryon).

OLIVA ISPIDULA, *Linn*, Sow., Thes. Conch., vol. iv., p 21, pl. 343, fig. 248 — Knysna.

OLIVA SCITULA, *Marrat*, Sow., Thes. Conch., vol. vi., pl. 333, fig. 76.—Durban.

ANCILLA DECIPIENS, Sowerby, n. sp. (pl. 6, fig. 23). Testa oblongo-ovata, crassa, pallide purpurascens, antice et postice fusco fasciata ; spira mediocriter elata, obtusiuscula ; anfractus 6, planato convexi ; callo tenui obtecti ; callositate polita, fusco fulvoque zonata ; anfractus ultimus convexius culus, haud angulatus ; columella arcuata, callosa, purpurea, superne callo fusco latemarginato effuso ; apertura oblongo-ovalis, intus purpurea.
Long. 28, diam 15 millim.
Hab , Port Elizabeth.
Allied to *A. obtusa* and *australis*, but distinct from both.

ANCILLA CONTUSA, *Reeve*, Conch Icon. (*Ancillaria*), pl. ix , fig. 31.—Durban.

ANCILLA OPTIMA, *Sowerby*, n. sp (Plate vi., fig. 31). Testa subfusiformi-ovata. solidiuscula pallide fulvo-carnea, longitudinaliter sparsim rufescente strigata, antice et postice vivide fusco fasciata ; spira mediocriter elata, acutiuscula : anfractus 6, planato-convexi, callo tenui obtecti ; callositate polita, fusco fulvoque balteata ; anfractus ultimus con-vexiusculus, superne obtusissime angulatus, liris obliquis numerosis angustis instructus, infra angu um callo fusco sulca alba marginato, infra medium zona angusta alba, sulca vix profunda marginata, cinctus ; ad basin varice calloso fusco unisulcato terminante ; columella alba, polita, levissime contorta, extus biplicata, superne callo albo effuso ; apertura latiuscula, alba.
Long. 38. maj. diam. 21 millim.
Hab. Durban.
Of this fine species, I have at present only seen two specimens. It is allied to *A. australis* and *A. obtusa*, from both ot which. however it differs very materially. It may be readily distinguished from its congeners, by its acutely conical spire.

FASCIOLARIA TRAPEZIUM, *Linn*, Sowerby, Thes. Conch., vol. v., pl. 426, fig. 22.; var. AUDOUINI, *Jonas* (fig. 23.)—Durban.

FASCIOLARIA RUTILA, *Watson*, Voy Challenger, vol. xv., p. 242, pl. 13, fig. 6.—Off Cape of Good Hope 150 fath. This species bears a remarkable resemblance to *Sipho Islandicus*.

FASCIOLARIA FILAMENTOSA, *Chemnitz*, Sowerby, Thes. Conch., vol. v., pl. 424., fig. 9.—Natal.

LATIRUS ABNORMIS, *Sowerby* (Plate 6, fig. 7), Journal of Conchology, vol. vii., p. 6., 1894.—Natal.

LATIRUS TURRITUS, *Gmelin*, Tryon, Man. of Conch., vol. iii., p. 93, pl. 69, figs. 160, 161.—Natal.

PERISTERNIA FENESTRATA, *Gould*, Proc. Bost. Soc., vol. vii., p. 327.—Simon's Bay (Gould). A doubtful species, unfigured.

PERISTERNIA CROCEA, *Gray*, var. sulcata, Gray (*Turbinella*), Zool. Beechy's Voy. 116.—Natal.

VOLUTA FESTIVA, *Lamarck*, Sowerby, Thes. Conch., vol. i., pl. 52, figs. 79, 80.—A beautiful shell of great rarity. A young specimen in fair condition was found on the Natal coast by Mrs. Trotter.

MITRA LITERATA, *Lamarck*, Sowerby, Thes. Conch., vol. iv., pl. 372, fig. 436.—Natal.

MITRA CHINENSIS, *Gray*, Sowerby, Thes. Conch., vol iv., pl. 357, fig. 81.—Natal. A small specimen.

MITRA INTERLIRATA, *Reeve*, Conch. Icon. (*Mitra*), fig. 70.

MITRA CRENIFERA, *Lamarck*, Sowerby, Thes. Conch., vol. iv., pl. 354, fig. 30.—Durban.

MITRA TEXTURATA, *Lamarck*, Sowerby, Thes. Conch., vol. iv., pl. 358, fig. 84.—Durban.

MITRA CADAVEROSA. *Reeve*, Proc. Zool. Soc. 1844, Sowerby, Thes. Conch., vol. iv., pl 370, fig 386.—Durban.

MITRA EXASPERATA, *Gmelin*, Sowerby, Thes. Conch, vol. iv. pl. 371, fig. 419.—Durban.

MITRA CIRCULATA, *Kiener*, Sowerby, Thes. Conch., vol. iv., pl. 358, fig. 86.—Durban.

MITRA FLAMMEA, *Quoy*, Sowerby, Thes. Conch., vol. iv., pl. 262, fig. 173.—Durban.

MITRA RUFESCENS, *A. Adams*, Proc. Zool. Soc. 1851, p. 137.—Durban. I doubt whether this is specifically distinct from *M. circulata*. The body whorl is more cylindrical.

MITRA PRETIOSA, *Reeve*, Sowerby, Thes. Conch., vol. iv., pl. 14, fig. 236.—Natal.

MITRA BOVEI, *Kiener*, Sowerby, Thes. Conch., vol. iv., pl. 5, fig. 60.—Natal (Gibbons).

MITRA LUCTUOSA, *A. Adams*, Sowerby, Thes. Conch., vol. iv., pl. 14, fig. 229.—Durban.

MITRA CINNAMOMEA, *A. Adams* (*Volutomitra*), Proc. Zool. Soc. 1854, p. 134 —Natal (Adams).

MITRA ZEPHYRINA, *Duclos*, Sowerby, Thes. Conch., vol. iv., pl. 18, fig. 306.—Durban.

MITRA FUSCESCENS, *Pease*, Sow., Thes. Conch., vol. v., pl. 367, fig. 303.—Durban.

MARGINELLA BENSONI, *Reeve*, Conch. Icon., fig. 151.—Algoa Bay (Gibbons).

MARGINELLA LUCIDA, *Marrat*, Journ. of Conch., vol. i., p. 205. Tryon, vol. v., pl 12, fig. 25.—Algoa Bay (Gibbons). This appears scarcely to differ from *M. pellicula* of the same author.

MARGINELLA CINEREA, *Jousseaume*, Reeve. Conch. Icon. (Marginella), sp. 145.—(*M. semen*, Reeve, non Lea).

MARGINELLA PUELLA, *Gould*, Proc. Bost. Soc, vol. 7, p. 385.—Simon's Bay (Gould). Unfigured, and unknown to me.

MARGINELLA QUADRIFASCIATA, *Marrat*, Ann. and Mag. Nat. Hist. 4th Series, vol. xii., p. 426 (unfigured).—S. Africa.

MARGINELLA ALBANYANA, *Gaskoin*, Ann. and Mag. Nat. Hist. 2 Series, vol. xi., p. 104.—Albany (Gaskoin). Unknown to me.

MARGINELLA RUFULA, *Gaskoin*, Reeve, Conch. Icon. (Marginella), fig. 149.—Green Point.

MARGINELLA PERMINIMA, *Sowerby* (pl. 6, fig. 36), Journal of Conchology, vol. vii., p. 7.—S. Africa (Turton).

MARGINELLA BURNUPI, *Sowerby*, n. sp. (pl. 6, fig. 35). Testa cylindrica, alba, solidiuscula ; spira fere plana ; apertura angusta ; columella quinqueplicata ; plicis acutis ; labrum crassiusculum.

Long. 4, diam. 2 millim.

Hab. Port Elizabeth.

A small cylindrical white shell with the spire almost flat.

MARGINELLA PONSONBYI, *Sowerby*, n. sp. (pl. 6, fig. 2). Testa subcylindrica, nitens, sub-pellucida, pallide cornea, strigis fulvis transversis irregulariter ornata ; antice leviter attenuata, postice vix inflata ; spira obtuse conica, parum elevata ; apertura angustiuscula, antice paulo latior ; columella triplicata ; labrum incrassatum.

Hab. S. Africa.

Long. 9, diam. 5 millim.

A sub-pellucid shell of somewhat cylindrical form, pale in colour with transverse fulvous streaks, some of which run obliquely.

COLUMBELLA FULMINATA, *Gould*, " Otia," p. 131.—Simon's Bay (Stimpson).

COLUMBELLA OBTUSA, *Sowerby*, Thes. Conch., vol. i., p. 120, pl. 37, fig. 63.—Durban.

COLUMBELLA PYRAMIDALIS, *Sowerby* (pl. 6, fig. 4), Journal of Conchology, vol. vii. p. 7.—Port Elizabeth.

COLUMBELLA KITCHINGI, *Sowerby*, pl. 6, fig. 3, Journal of Conchology, vol. vii., p. 7. – Green Point, Cape of Good Hope.

COLUMBELLA MERCATORIA, *Lamarck*, Sow., Thes. Conch , vol. i., p. 115, pl. 36, figs. 28-32.—Natal. Very common in the West Indies.

COLUMBELLA LIGULA, *Duclos*, Monog., pl. 2, figs. 11-16, Sow , Thes. Conch. vol. i. p. 123. pl. 38, figs. 83-85.—Natal (Gibbons). Is. Ticao (Cuming), Solomon Islands, and Australia.

COLUMBELLA AVENA, *Reeve*. Conch. Icon. (*Columbella*), fig. 158.—Buffalo, Cape Colony (Reeve).

COLUMBELLA LANGLEYI, n. sp. (pl. 8, f. 8, 9).—Testa elongata, pellucida, succinacea, polita ; spira acuminata, acutiuscula, ad apicem obtusa ; anfractus 5, convexi, longitudinaliter obscurissime plicati, superne obtusissime angulati ; ultimus spiram fere æquans, leviter inflata, basim versus leviter attenuatus ; apertura oblonga ; columella levissime contorta ; labrum tenue.

Long. 4.50, diam. 1.50 millim.
Hab. Port Elizabeth (Crawford).
A smooth, transparent, amber-coloured little shell.

COLUMBELLA CONSANGUINEA, n. sp. (pl. viii. f. 6, 7). Testa elongata, fulvo fusca, crassiuscula, undique sculpta ; spira acuminata, ad apicem obtusa; anfractus 5, convexi, rotundati, spiraliter striati, longitudinaliter plicati, plicis pernumerosis, interstitiis puncturatis; anfractus ultimus spiram paulo superans, basim versus leviter attenuatus : apertura oblonga ; columella rectiuscula, labrum leviter incrassatum.
Long. 4.25, diam. 1.50 millim.
Hab. Port Elizabeth.
Similar in form to *C. Langleyi*, but of a thicker substance, and sculptured with fine, close, longitudinal riblets, and minute spiral striæ.

ENGINA NATALENSIS, *Melvill*, Proc. Malac. Soc., vol. i , p. 226.—Durban.

HARPA VENTRICOSA, *Lamarck*, Sow., Thes. Conch., vol. iii., p. 169, pl. 232, figs. 18, 22.—Durban.

CASSIS GLAUCA, *Lamarck*, Reeve, Conch. Icon. (*Cassis*), fig. 33.—Natal. Common in the Indian Ocean.

CASSIS AREOLA, *Lamarck*, Reeve, Conch. Icon. (*Cassis*), fig. 24.—Durban. Widely distributed in the Indian and Pacific Oceans.

CASSIS BISULCATA, *Schub & Wagn.*, Reeve, Conch. Icon. (*Cassis*), fig. 6.—Natal.

CASSIS PILA, *Reeve*, Conch. Icon. (*Cassis*), fig. 31.—A variety without blotches, specimen in perfect condition, found at Durban.

CASSIS CRATICULATUS, *Euthyme*, Bull. Soc. Mal. de France, vol. ii., p. 250 (unfigured). I think from the description that this is *C. pila*.—S. Africa.

DOLIUM FIMBRIATUM, *Sowerby*, Reeve, Conch. Icon. (*Dolium*) fig. 3.—Durban.

DOLIUM PROCELLARUM, *Euthyme*, Bull. de la Soc. Mal. de France, vol. ii., p. 247.—Pt. Elizabeth (Euthyme). Having read the description (without figure) I feel almost sure that this is the same as *D. luteostoma*.

PYRULA FICUS, *Linn.*, Sow., Thes. Conch., vol. iv., pl. 423, fig. 4.—Natal.

PYRULAFICOIDES, *Lamarck*, Tryon, Man. of Conch., vol. vii., pl. v., fig. 28. P. reticulata, auctorum, sed non Lamk.—Durban.

NATICA QUEKETTI, *Sowerby* (pl. 6, fig. 6), Journal of Conch., vol. vii., p. 8.—Natal.

NATICA SEBA*, *Souleyet*, Voy. de la Bonite, pl. 35, figs. 6, 7.—Thes. Conch., vol. v., pl. 457, fig. 79.—Natal.

NATICA TÆNIATA, *Menke* (N. *ala-papilionis*, Ch.), Sow., Thes. Conch., vol. v., pl. 457, fig. 4.—Natal.

NATICA ZANZIBARICA, *Recluz*, Sow., Thes. Conch., vol. v., pl. 457, fig. 73. (A young specimen).—Durban.

NATICA MELANOSTOMA, *Gmelin*, Sow., Thes Conch., vol. iv., pl. 457, fig. 72.—Durban.

NATICA SIMPLEX, *Sow.*, n. sp., pl. 6, fig. 18.—Testa parva, gibbosa, alba, lævis, aut obscure longitudinaliter sculpta; spira breviter conica; anfractus 4, convexi, sutura vix impressa; anfractus ultimus rotundatus; columella rectiuscula, callosa; umbilicus parvus, angustus; apertura mediocriter lata, fauce alba, lævis.
Long. 6, diam. 5.50 millim.
Hab. South Africa (Turton).
A small white shell of very simple and regular form.

NATICINA PAPILLA, *Gmelin*, Tryon, Man. of Conch., vol. 8, pl. 25, fig. 87.—Durban.

SIGARETUS PLANULATUS, *Recluz*, Thes. Conch., vol. v., pl. 442, fig. 29.—Durban.

SIGARETUS DELESSERTI, *Recluz*, Sow., Thes. Conch., vol. v., pl. 442, figs. 20-22.—Durban.

VANIKORO DESHAYESIANA, *Recl.*, Sow., Thes. Conch., vol. v., pl. 482, fig. 17.—Durban.

SCALARIA JUKESIANA, *Forbes*, Voy. Rattlesnake, Append, p. 383, pl. 3, fig. 7.—Port Elizabeth.

SCALARIA SIMPLEX, Sow. (pl. 6, fig. 5), Journal of Conchology, vol. vii., p. 8, 1894.—Natal.

TEREBRA RUFOPUNCTATA, *Smith*, Ann. and Mag. of Nat. Hist., 1877, vol. xix., p. 29.—Durban.

TEREBRA DIMIDIATA, *Lamk.*, Sow., Thes. Conch., vol. i., pl. 41, fig. 7, 8.—Durban.

TEREBRA CASTA, *Hinds*, Sow., Thes. Conch., vol. i., pl. 44, fig. 84.—Natal.

TEREBRA STRAMINEA, *Gray*, Sow., Thes. Conch. vol. i., pl. 42, fig. 22, 23.— Natal.

TEREBRA LÆVIGATA, *Gray*, Sow., Thes. Conch., vol. i., pl. 44, fig. 93.—Natal.

TEREBRA LONGISCATA, *Deshayes*, Reeve, Conch. Icon., fig. 103.— Durban.

TEREBRA FICTILIS, *Hinds*, Sow., Thes. Conch. vol. i., pl. 45, f. 109, 110.—Durban.

TEREBRA GEMINATA, *Deshayes*, Proc. Zool. Soc. 1859, p. 296 (unfigured).—Natal (Deshayes). Probably var. of *T. spectabilis*, Hinds.

TEREBRA NEBULOSA, *Sowerby*, Thes Conch., vol. i , pl. 43, fig. 51. (?...*T. nubeculata*, Sow.)—Durban.

TEREBRA BABYLONIA, *Lamarck*, Sow., Thes. Conch., vol. i., pl. 43, fig. 67.—Durban.

TEREBRA SUBULATA, *Lamarck*, Sow., Thes. Conch., vol. i., pl. 41, fig. 16.—Durban.

PYRAMIDELLA MITRALIS, A. Adams, Sow., Thes. Conch , vol. ii., p. 814, pl. 172, fig. 9.—Durban.

OBELISCUS TERES, *A. Adams*, Sow., Thes. Conch., vol. ii., p. 807, pl. 171, f. 31, 32.—Durban.

OBELISCUS DOLABRATUS, *Linn.*, Sow., Thes. Conch., vol. ii., pl. 171, fig. 1.—Durban.

CIONISCUS UNILINEATUS, *Sowerby* (Plate 6., fig. 8), Journal of Conchology, vol. vii., p. 8 (as *Aclis*).—Port Elizabeth.

CIONISCUS PELLUCIDUS, *Sowerby* n. sp. (Plate 6, fig. 10). Testa parva, turrita, alba, pellucida ; anfractus 6½, convexi, spiraliter subtilissime striati, liris tenuissimis 2-3, superne instructi ; sutura impressa, anguste lirata ; nucleus sub-retrorsus ; anfractus ultimus ¼ longitudinis æquans, leviter rotundatus ; apertura ovata ; labrum tenue ; columella tenuissima, leviter incurvata, haud plicata.

Long. 3.50. diam. 1.50 millim.

Hab. Port Elizabeth.

A little white pellucid shell, very lightly spirally striated ; whorls slightly shouldered, with two or three fine ridges.

TURBONILLA TROCHLEARIS, *Gould* (Chemnitzia), Otia Conchologica, p. 151 (unfigured).—Simon's Bay (Gould).

TURBONILLA OBELISCUS, *Gould* (Chemnitzia), Otia Conchologica, p. 150 (unfigured).—Simon's Bay.

EULIMA SIMPLEX, *Sowerby*, n. sp. (Plate 6, fig. 9.)   Testa subulata, polita, semipellucida, alba ; spira acutiuscula, ad apicem obtusa ; anfractus 7, vix convexi ; anfr. ultimus ⅓ longitudinis æquans ; apertura ovata, leviter obliqua ; columella oblique rectiuscula.
Long. 3.50, diam. 1.50. millim.
Hab. South Africa.
A little white species of very simple character.

ODOSTOMIA LUCIDA, *Sowerby*, n. s.p. (Plate 6, fig. 11). Testa oblonga, alba, subpellucida, lævis, antice inflata, postice acuminata ; spira mediocriter elongata, convexiuscula ; anfractus 5, convexiusculi ; sutura impressa, lira angusta inserta ; anfractus ultimus spiram æquans, basin versus inflatus, rotundatus ; apertura ovata ; columella leviter sinuata.
Long. 3, diam. 1½ millim.
Hab. Port Elizabeth.

CERITHIOPSIS LIRATA, *Sowerby*, n. sp. (Plate 6, fig. 12). Testa elongato pyramidalis, fulva, antice angulata ; spira acuta, ad apicem obtusiuscula ; anfractus 11, primi 3 læves, rotundati, sequentes planati, spiraliter tri-lirati ; sutura vix conspicua ; anfractus ultimus brevis, quadriliratus ; basis concava, lira unica marginata ; columella brevis, rectiuscula, apertura quadrata.
Long. 4.25, diam. 1.75.
Hab. Port Elizabeth.
A little shell of very distinct pyramidal form, with a flattened, slightly concave base.   The spiral ridges are like those prevailing in the genus *Turritella*.

CERITHIOPSIS EXQUISITA, *Sowerby*, n. sp. (Plate 6, fig. 13). Testa turricula, fulva ; spira convexiuscula, ad apicem acuta ; anfractus 10, primi minuti, læves, sequentes convexi, biangulati, liris spiralibus et longitudinalibus decussatim exigue sculpta ; sutura impressa, lira angusta munita ; anfractus ultimus breviusculus superne leviter concavus, ad basin convexiusculus, anguste umbilicatus ; columella brevis, rectiuscula, apertura subquadrata.
Long. 4.50, diam. 1.50 millim.
Hab. Natal.
A fulvous crisply sculptured little shell.

SOLARIUM MAXIMUM, *Philippi*, Sow., Thes. Conch vol iii., pl. 250, figs. 5-6.—Durban. Usually found in the China Sea.

SOLARIUM LÆVIGATUM, *Lamarck*, Sow., Thes. Conch.. vol. iii., pl. 251, figs. 21-22.—Durban, Persian Gulf, Indian Ocean, &c.

SOLARIUM PERSPECTIVUM, *Linn.*, Sow., Thes. Conch. vol. iii., pl. 253, figs. 36-38.—Natal, and Indian and Pacific Oceans.

SOLARIUM (PHILIPPIA) HYBRIDUM, *Linn.*, Sow., Thes. Conch., vol. iii, pl. 253, fig. 39 —St. John's (Turton).

SOLARIUM (TORINIA) DORSUOSUM, *Hinds*, Sow., Thes. Conch., vol. iii, pl. 254. fig. 73.—St. John's (Turton), Natal. Also Persian Gulf, and Japan.

SOLARIUM (TORINIA) CYLINDRACEUM, *Chemnitz*, Sow., Thes. Conch., vol. iii., pl. 254, figs. 98, 99.—Natal.

IANTHINA PALLIDA, *Harvey*, Sow., Thes. Conch., vol. v., pl. 444, figs. 19, 20.—Port Elizabeth.

CONUS CEYLANENSIS, *Hwass*, Sow., Thes. Conch., vol. iii., pl. 192, figs. 139-41.—Durban.

CONUS QUERCINUS, *Bruguiere*, Sow., Thes. Conch., vol. iii., pl. 197, fig. 239.—Natal. Common in the Indian Ocean, Persian Gulf, East Africa, &c.

CONUS MILES, *Linn.*, Sow., Thes. Conch., vol. iii., pl. 193, fig. 157.—Durban. Widely distributed, principally in the Indian Ocean.

CONUS VERMICULATUS, *Lamarck*, Sow., Thes. Conch. vol. iii., pl. 189 fig. 52.—Durban. Distr., N.E. Africa, Red Sea, Indian Ocean, &c.

CONUS LEGATUS, *Lamarck*, Sow., Thes. Conch., vol. iii., pl. 209, fig. 566 (*C. musivus*, Brod).— Natal (Gibbons).

CONUS LAMARCKI. *Kiener*, Coq. Viv., p. 240, pl. 83, fig. 4.— S. Africa (Tryon).

CONUS PRIMULA, *Reeve*, Conch. Icon. Supp., pl. 6, fig. 259.— Natal (Tryon).

CONUS PLUMBEUS, *Reeve*, Conch. Icon. (*Conus*), fig. 253.— S. Africa (Tryon).

CONUS RATTUS. *Lamarck*, Sow., Thes. Conch., vol. iii., pl. 193, fig. 161.—Durban.

CONUS ARACHNOIDEUS, *Gmelin*, Sow., Thes. Conch., vol. iii., pl. 1, fig. 14.—Natal.

CONUS ARENATUS, *Hwass*, Sow., Thes. Conch., vol. iii., pl. 188, fig. 7.—Durban.

CONUS OBSCURUS, *Humph.* Sow., Thes. Conch., vol. iii., pl. 208, fig. 526.—Durban.

STROMBUS FUSIFORMIS, *Sowerby*, Thes. Conch., vol. i., pl. 9. figs. 91, 92.—Durban.

CYPRÆA CLANDESTINA, *Linn.*, Sow., Thes. Conch., vol. iv., pl. 310, f. 139.—Durban.

CYPRÆA STERCUS-MUSCARUM, *Lamarck*, Sow., Thes. Conch., vol. iv., pl. 323, f. 363 —Natal (Gibbons).

CYPRÆA CASTANEA, *Higgins*, Sow., Thes. Conch., vol. iv., pl. 320, figs. 302, 303.—Cape of Good Hope (Higgins).

CYPRÆA CRIBRARIA, *Linn*, Sow., Thes. Conch., vol. iv., pl. 311, fig. 164.—Umzinto, Natal.

CYPRÆA STAPHYLÆA, *Linn*, Sow , Thes. Conch., vol. iv., pl. 316, fig. 225. (var. *Limacina*, Lam.)

TRIVIA PRODUCTA, *Gaskoin*, Sow., Thes. Conch., vol. iv., pl. 327, f. 495.—Agulhas Bank.

TRIVIA SULCATA, *Gaskoin*, Sow., Thes. Conch., vol. iv., pl. 326, f. 454.—Pondoland (Layard).

TRIVIA QUADRIPUNCTATA, *Gray*, Sow., Thes. Conch., vol. iv., pl. 326, f. 460.—Pondoland (Layard). Common in West Indies, also reported from Philippines.

TRIVIA INSECTA, *Mighels*, Sow., Thes. Conch., vol. iv., pl. 326, fig 478.—S. Africa.

TRIVIA ORYZA, *Lamarck*, Sow., Thes. Conch., vol. iv., pl. 326, fig. 474.—Durban.

TRIVIA VITREA, *Gaskoin*, Sow., Thes. Conch., vol. iv., pl. 326, fig. 456.—Durban.

CANCELLARIA IMBRICATA, *Watson*, Linn. Soc. Journ. Zool. xvi., p. 325. Moll. Voy. Challenger vol. xv., pl. 18, fig. 10.— Off Cape of Good Hope (Watson).

CERITHIUM CRASSILABRUM, *Krauss*, Sow., Thes. Conch., vol. ii., pl. 182, f. 203.—Durban.

Pyrazus palustris, *Linn.*, Sow., Thes. Conch., vol. ii., pl. 185, f. 261.—Natal.

Triforis corrugatus, *Hinds.* Tryon, Man. of Conch., vol. ix., pl. 39, f. 59.—Durban.

Rissoa (Cingula) caffra, n. sp. (Plate 6, fig. 15.) Testa ovato-conoidea, anguste umbilicata, tenuis, polita, fulvo-cornea, fusco obscure trifasciata; spira conica; anfractus 5, convexi; sutura profunda; anfractus ultimus spiram superans, inflata, rotundata; apertura ovata, peristoma simplex.

Long. 2.50, diam. 1.50 millim.

Hab. Port Elizabeth.

A thin, polished, horny little shell with three faint bands.

Turritella declivis, *Adams & Reeve,* Voy. of Samarang, Moll. p. 48, pl. 2, fig. 10.—Hout's Bay.

Xenophora corrugata, *Reeve,* Conch. Icon., sp. 6.—Durban.

Calyptra cicatricosa, *Reeve,* Conch. Icon. (Calyptræa), fig. 3.—Durban.

Calyptra porosa, *Reeve,* Conch. Icon. (Calyptræa), fig. 20.—Durban.

Turbo intercostalis, *Menke,* Sow., Thes. Conch., vol. v., pl. 494. f. 14.—Durban.

Turbo (Leptothyra) pillula. *Dunker,* Sow., Thes Conch., vol. 5, pl. 505, f. 160.—St. John's (Turton).

Turbo tricarinulatus, *Euthyme,* Bull. de la Soc. Malac de France, vol. ii., p. 252. (unfigured). This is surely a small form of *T. cidaris,* with the keels of var. *nataleusis* (Reeve).

Turbo Ponsonbyi, n. sp. (Plate 6, fig. 20.) Testa subglobosa, crassa, profunde umbilicata, grisea, fusco maculata, spiraliter dense lirata; liris rotundatis, maculis parvis fuscis articulatis, lira minima interveniente; spira breviter conica; anfractus 4, convexi; sutura canaliculata; anfr. ultimus rotundatus; basis convexa, costa crassa nodosa in regione umbilicali, sulca profunda et latiuscula marginata, instructa; apertura fere circularis, fauce alba; peristoma crassum. Operculum intus planum, extus convexum, profunde umbilicatum, corrugatum, carina angustiuscula marginatum.

Long 8, diam. 8 millim.
Hab. Durban.
A small shell resembling one of the larger species of
Leptothyra (*Collonia*), from which section it differs principally
in the form of its operculum.

PACHYPOMA TAYLORIANUM, *Smith*, Proc. Zool. Soc. 1880,
pl. 48, fig. 9, p. 483.—Port Elizabeth.   This species was
described from a single specimen without locality in the
collection of the late Thos. Lombe Taylor.

GIBBULA TRYONI, *Pilsbry* (Plate 6, fig. 22.) Manual of
Conchology, vol. xi., p. 239, pl. 69, figs. 20, 21.   *G. incincta*,
Sow. Journ. of Conch., April 1894, is a synonym.

GIBBULA FUCATA, Gould, Proc. Boston Soc. Nat. Hist.
p. 8, p. 20.—Simon's Bay (Turton).

GIBBULA LOCULOSA, *Gould*, '' Otia," p. 159.—False Bay.

MARGARITA PINTADO, *Gould*, " Otia," p. 154.—Simon's
Bay.

MARGARITA ARTICULATA, *Gould*, " Otia," p. 154.—Simon's
Bay.

MONILEA SPURIA, *Gould*, " Otia," p. 155.—Simon's Bay.

SOLARIELLA SPLENDENS, *Sowerby*, n. sp. (pl. 6, fig. 21).—
Testa depresse orbicularis, late et profunde umbilicata, aureo-
nitens, fusco maculata ad basim fusco oblique strigata; spira
breviter conica, gradata, ad apicem acuta ; anfractus 6½
tabulati, spiraliter grano-lirati, sutura canaliculata sejuncti ;
anfractus ultimus depresse rotundatus, supra angulatus,
infra rotundatus, liris 7, suprenis granulatis, cœteris planis ;
basis convexa, lævis ; umbilicus perspectivus, intus grano-
liratus; apertura sub-quadrata, vix obliqua; columella oblique
rectiuscula, vix callosa.
Alt. 6, diam. 9 millim.
Hab. Natal.
A pretty little shining shell, smooth below and with
about 7 ridges above the periphery, the upper ridges being
beaded.

CALLIOSTOMA LAYARDI, Sowerby, n. sp. (pl. 8, f. 10, 11).
Testa conica, clatiuscula, angustissime umbilicata, argenteo-
nitens, ad angulum vivide rubro bicingulata, ad basim rubra ;
spira acuta, ad apicem vivide rubra ; anfractus 6½, primi (2)
læves rotundati, sequentes plano declives, liris 4 leviter
nodulosis instructi, ad angulum rubro bicarinati; sutura

canaliculata ; basis vix convexa, valde lirata, liris 7-8 con-
fertiusculis, rotundatis ; columella leviter obliqua, callosa ;
apertura oblique sub-quadrata, intus argentea.

Alt. 13, diam. 14 millim.

Hab. Pondoland (Layard).

A regularly conical typical *Calliostoma*, distinguished by
the bright ruby double keel at the angle of the whorls. In
the type specimen the narrow umbilicus is only partially
covered, but probably in older shells it would be entirely
closed.

CLANCULUS KRAUSSI, *Philipti* (*Monodonta*), Conch. Cab.,
p. 82, pl. 14, f. 14.—Durban.

EUCHELUS QUADRICARINATUS, *Chemnitz* (*Trochus*), Conch.
Cab. xi., p. 167, pl. 196, f. 1892.—Durban.

UMBONIUM VESTIARIUM, *Linn.*, Sow., Thes. Conch.,
vol. v., pl. 472, figs. 1-5.—Durban.

FISSURELLA SIMILIS, *Sowerby*, Thes. Conch., vol. iii.,
p. 194, pl. 241, f 143.—Durban

FISSURELLA GRÆCA, *Linn.*, Sow., Illust. Index Brit. Shells,
pl. 11, figs. 1, 2 (F. reticulata, Donov).—Durban.

MACROCHISMA COMPRESSA, *A. Adams*, Sow., Thes. Conch.,
vol iii., p. 205, pl 244, f. 218.—S Africa Turton).

CHITON LYRATUS, *Sowerby*, Conch. Illust., fig. 126.—Port
Elizabeth.

CHITON (ISCHNOCHITON) ELIZABETHENSIS, *Pilsbry*. "The
Nautilus," vol. viii., p. 9.—Port Elizabeth. This is the species
quoted by me as *Chiton marginatus*, which it very closely
resembles. Mr. E. R. Sykes (Proc. Malac. Soc., vol. i., p.
133) expressed the opinion that it was identical with *C. oniscus*,
Krauss.

CHITON (ACANTHOPLEURA) AFRA, *Rochebrune*, Bull, Soc.
Philom. 1882. p. 192.—Cape of Good Hope (Verreaux).
Unknown to me.

CHITON (ACANTHOPLEURA) QUATREFAGESI, *Rochebrune*,
Journ. de Conch, 1881, p. 44.—Cape of Good Hope (Verreaux).
Unknown to me.

CHITON (ACANTHOCHITES) CARPENTERI, *Pilsbry*, Man. of
Conch., vol. xv., p 35, pl. 1, f. 14-22.—Pt. Elizabeth.

CHITON (ONITHOCHITON) LITERATUS, *Krauss*, sudafrik, Moll., p. 36.--Natal (Krauss).

CHITON (ONITHOCHITON) ALVEOLATUS, *Rochebrune*, Bull. Soc. Phil. de Paris, 1883, p. 32.—Cape of Good Hope (Paris Museum).

CHITON (GYMNOPLAX) ANAGLYPTUS, *Rochebrune*, Bull. Soc. Phil. de Paris, 1883, p. 33.—Cape of Good Hope (Paris Museum.)

CHITON (GYMNOPLAX) MELANOTREPHUS, *Rochebrune*, Bull. Soc. Phil. de Paris, 1883, p. 34.—Cape of Good Hope (Paris Museum).

ACTÆON FLAMMEUS, *Gmelin*, Reeve, Conch. Icon. (Tornatella) fig 2.—Durban.

ACTÆON (SOLIDULA) AFFINIS, *A. Adams*, Proc. Zool. Soc., 1854, p. 61.—Pilsbry, Man. of Conch., vol. xv., pl. 20 A, fig. 52.—Durban.

HYDATINA UNDATA, *Bruguière*, Pilsbry, Man. of Conch., vol. xv., pl. 59., f. 20, 21.—Natal.

BULLINA OBLONGA, Sowerby, n. sp. (plate 8, fig. 12, 13). Testa oblongo-ovalis, postice acuminata, antice leviter attenuata, undique confertim sulcata, grisea, fusco tri-zonata, strigis numerosis fuscis irregularibus ornata; spira elatiuscula, convexa, ad apicem acuta; anfractus 4½, rotunde convexi; sutura anguste canaliculata; anfr. ultimus elongatus, superne leviter rotundatus; apertura oblonga, mediocriter lata, utrinque angustior; labrum tenue, columella rectiuscula, obscurissime plicata.

Long. 13, diam. 7 millim
Hab. Pondoland (Layard)
Compared with *B. Ziczac* the spire is much higher.

HAMINEA GRACILIS, *Sowerby*, n. sp. (Pl. 6, fig. 16.) Testa anguste rimata, oblongo sub-cylindracea, tenuis, pallide straminea, antice mediocriter lata, postice angustior, undique spiraliter minutissime striata, longitudinaliter leviter et irregulariter plicata; vertice anguste sed profunde umbilicata; apertura antice lata, postice angusta.

Long. 11 diam, 6.50 millim.
Hab. Durban.

APLUSATRUM AMPLUSTRE, *Linn.*, Pilsbry, Man. of Conch. vol. xv., pl. 44, figs. 1-6. Synonyms, *Bulla aplustre*, Lamk. *Aplustrum fasciatum*, Schum., *Aplustra pulchella*, Swains.

Amplustre thalassiarchi, Martini, &c.—Durban. A species of wide geographical distribution.

ATYS ELONGATA, *A. Adams* (Bulla), Sow., Thes. Conch., vol. ii., pl. 125, f. 121.—Durban. Widely distributed in the Indian and Pacific Oceans.

CYLINDROBULLA SCULPTA, *G. & H. Nevill*, Journ. Asiatic Soc., p. 2, No. 2, 1869, p. 68, pl. 13, fig. 3.—Hab., Port Elizabeth.

VOLVATELLA LAGUNCULA, *Sowerby* (pl. 6, fig. 17), Journa of Conchology, vol. vii., p. 10., 1894.—Port Elizabeth.

PELECYPODA.

SOLEN CORNEUS, *Lamarck*, Scw., Conch. Icon. (*Solen*), fig. 19.—Durban.

SOLEN SLOANEI, *Gray*, Sow., Conch. Icon., f. 10.—Durban.

PANDORA DISSIMILIS, *Sowerby* (pl. 6, fig. 33), Journal of Conchology, vol. vii., p. 11, April, 1894.—Sea Point, Cape Town.

BASTEROTIA OBTUSA, *Sowerby* (pl. 6, fig. 27), Journal of Conchology, vol. vi., p. 11, April, 1894.—Durban.

BASTEROTIA TRICOSTALIS, *Sowerby*, n. sp. (pl. 8, figs. 14, 15. — Testa æquivalvis, inæquilateralis, pallide straminea, elongato-subtrigona, crassiuscula. antice breviuscula, rotundata, postice longior, oblique, declivis, angulata, ad angulum acute carinata, irregulariter rugosa ; area postica leviter concava, valde tricostalis; umbones acuti, approximati, lunula parva ; cardo in utraque valva dentem unicum leviter excurvatum munitus.

Antero-post 12, umbono marg. 7 millim.

Hab. Durban (Burnup).

This second species of *Basterotia*, which I have described from South Africa, is more like the type of the genus than the first (*B. obtusa*). It has a prominent keel ridge at the posterior angle, behind which the somewhat concave area is furnished with two additional keels or ribs.

MACTRA ACHATINA, *Chemnitz*, Conch. Cab. vol. ii., p. 218, fig. 1957.—Reeve, Conch. Icon. (*Mactra*), fig. 51.

MACTRA ÆQUISULCATA, *Sowerby* (pl. 8, fig. 26), Journal of Conchology, vol. vii., p. 12.—Durban.

RAETA PELLICULA, *Deshayes*, Reeve, Conch. Icon. (*Mactra*), pl. 21. fig. 124.—Durban.

MACTRINULA OVALINA, *Lamk*, Reeve, Conch. Icon.(*Mactra*), fig. 66 (=*depressa*, Speng).—Durban.

SEMELE CORDIFORMIS, *Chemnitz*, Reeve, Conch. Icon. (*Amphidesma*), pl. 5, fig. 30.—Natal.

IACRA SEYCHELLARUM, *H. & A. Adams*, Rec. Moll. vol. ii., p. 409.—Natal.

PSAMMOBIA BURNUPI, *Sowerby* (plate 6, fig. 30), Journal of Conchology, vol. vii., p. 12, 1894.

PSAMMOBIA ORNATA, *Deshayes*, Reeve, Conch. Icon. (*Psammobia*), fig. 36.—Durban.

TELLINA DISPAR, *Conrad*, Sow., Thes. Conch. vol. i., p. 306, pl. 59, fig. 108.—Natal.

TELLINA VIRGATA,*Linn.*, Sow., Thes. Conch., vol. i., p. 228, pl. 65, fig. 212.—Natal.

TELLINA RASTELLUM, *Hanley*, Sow., Thes. Conch., vol. i., p. 223, pl. 64, fig. 231.—Natal.

TELLINA PLANISSIMA, *Anton*, Sow., Thes. Conch., vol. i., p. 295, pl. 59, fig. 124.—Durban.

TELLINA PHARAONIS, *Hanley*, Sow., Thes. Conch., vol. i., p. 235, pl. 63, f. 215.—Durban.

TELLINA PERNA, *Spengler*, Sow., Thes. Conch. vol. i., p. 236, pl. 63, f. 202.—Natal.

TELLINA QUEKETTI, n. sp. (plate 8, fig. 16.)   Testa trigono sub-ovalis, solidiuscula, inæquilateralis, alba, nitens, concentrice levissime rugata ; umbones leviter prominentes, acutiusculi, post medium locati ; margo dorsalis utrinque declivis ; latus anticum rotundatum, posticum leviter truncatum, margo ventralis arcuatus.
Antero-post 15.50, umbono-marg. 11.50.
Hab. Durban.
Var. *radiata*. (fig. 17) Extus intusque purpureo radiata.

TELLINA VIRGULATA, *Hanley*, Sow., Thes. Conch , vol. i., pl. 56, fig. 5.—Durban.

TELLINA PRISMATICA, *Sowerby*, n. sp. (pl. vi., fig 29). Testa oblonga, tenuissima, compressa, iridescens, valde inæquilateralis, concentrice striata; margo dorsalis anticus leviter arcuatus, posticus valde declivis.

Antero-post 16, umbono-marg. 8 millim.

Hab. Durban.

A thin iridescent species, somewhat resembling *T. Valtonis*.

TELLINA VULSELLA, *Chemnitz*, Thes. Conch., vol. i., pl. 61, fig. 162.—Natal.

TELLINA (MACOMA) CANDIDATA, *Sowerby* (pl. vi., fig. 25), Journal of Conchology, vol. vii., p. 12, April 1894.—Durban.

STRIGILLIA TROTTERIANA, *Sowerby* (pl. 6, fig. 32), Journal of Conchology, vol. vii., p. 12, April, 1896.—Durban.

DONAX NITIDUS, *Deshayes*, Sow., Thes. Conch., vol. 3, p. 314, pl. 282, fig. 75.—Natal. Also East Australia.

DONAX LUBRICUS, *Hanley*, Reeve, "Conch. Icon." (*Donax*), pl. 7, fig. 46.—Natal.

DONAX ÆMULUS, *Smith*, Proc. Zool. Soc., 1877, p. 271, pl. 75, figs. 23-25.—Durban.

DONAX BURNUPI, *Sowerby* (pl. 6, fig. 26), Journal of Conchology, vol. vii., p. 14.—Natal.

DONAX SIMPLEX, *Sowerby*, n. sp. (pl. 8, fig. 18, 19). Testa cuneiformis solida, postice tumida, antice attenuata, luteo albida, radiatim striata; striis confertis, puncturatis, antice evanidis; umbones obtusi; margo dorsalis anticus oblique declivis, posticus sub rotunde truncatus, ventralis rectiusculus.

Antero-post 7, umbono-marg. 5, crass. 3 millim.

Hab. Umzinto, Natal.

This shell is somewhat similar to *D. æmulus* Smith, but the posterior side is more tumid and rounded.

DONAX FABA, *Chemnitz*, Sow., Thes. Conch., vol. iii., p. 312, plate 283, figs. 108, 109.—S. Africa.

CYTHEREA (TIVELA) TRANSVERSA, n. sp. (plate 7, figs. 2 and 3). Testa transverse oblonga, crassiuscula, leviter compressa, fere æquilateralis, utrinque leviter acuminata, læviuscula, nitens, albida, dilute fusco radiata et fasciata; umbones acutiusculi; margo dorsalis utrinque declivis, ventralis arcuatus; cardo normalis; pagina interna roseo tincta; impressiones musculares fuscia, sinu pallii producto.

Antero-post 59, umbono-marg. 42, crass. 24 millim.
Hab. Natal.
This species may be readily distinguished from its
congeners by its transversely oblong form.

CYTHEREA (TIVELA) ALUCINANS, *Sowerby*, n. sp. (plate 7,
figs. 5, 6.) Testa subtrigona, leviter inæquilateralis, crassa,
lævis, nitens, pallida, lineis fuscis angulatim undulatis parum
picta, epidermide tenui cornea induta ; umbones acutiusculi,
prominentes, paulo ante medium locati ; margo dorsalis
utrinque declivis, anticus rectiusculus, posticus leviter
arcuatus, ventralis arcuatus ; area postica planulata, antica
levissime concavo depressa ; pagina interna alba, postice
linea violacea picta ; impressiones musculares parviusculi,
sinu pallii lato paulo producto.
Antero-post 63, umbono-marg. 55 millim.
Hab. Natal.
A worn valve of this species was mistaken by me for
Meretrix zonaria (Journal of Conchology, vol. 7, p. 14.) I
have since seen fine fresh specimens, and find it to be a *Tivela*.

CYTHEREA (TIVELA) POLITA, *Sowerby*, Thes. Conch.,
vol. ii., p. 618, pl. 127, fig. 14.—Natal. *C. dolabella*, Sowerby,
is only a form of this species.

CYTHEREA (CARYATIS) MANILLÆ, *Sowerby*, Thes. Conch.,
vol. ii., p. 634, pl. 136, figs. 180, 181.—Natal.

CIRCE (CRISTA) DIVARICATA, *Chemnitz*, Sow.. Thes. Conch.,
vol. ii., p. 250, pl. 137, figs. 8, 9.—Natal.

LIOCONCHA PICTA, *Lamarck*, Sow., Thes. Conch.
(Cytherea), vol. ii., p. 642, pl. 134, f. 149.—Durban.

SUNETTA CONTEMPTA, *Smith*, Proc. Zool. Soc., 1891,
p. 422.—*Meröe menstrualis*, Reeve (non. Menke) Conch. Icon.,
vol. xiv., fig. 9.—Natal.

TAPES SULCARIA, *Lamarck*, Sow.. Thes. Conch., vol. ii.,
p. 685, pl. 146, f. 30-32.—Durban.

VENUS (CHIONE) LISTERI, *Gray*, Sow., Thes. Conch.,
vol. ii., p. 705, pl. 152, f. 7-9.—Durban.

VENUS (CHIONE) ARAKANA, *Nevill* (*Cryptogramma*), Journ.
Asiatic Soc., Bengal, vol. xxxix., part 2, p. 10, pl. 1, f. 16.—
Port Elizabeth and Durban.

VENUS (ANAITIS) LATILIRATA, Sowerby, n. sp. (pl. vi. fig.
24). Testa triangularis, crassa, liris concentricis latis

rotundatis et obsolete angulatis instructa, fulvescente alba, maculis numerosis parvis strigisque fuscis et carneo purpurascentibus radiata et aspersa ; umbones prominentes, complanati, ante medium locati ; latus anticum subtruncatum, posticum longius ; lunula parviuscula, area ligamenti late excavata.

Antero-post 25, umbono-marg, 20 millim.

Hab. Durban.

This shell has somewhat the appearance of the West-Indian *V. paphia*, but the ridges are not produced posteriorly into short laminæ as in that species.

✓ VENERUPIS LAJONKARI, *Payrandeau*, Sowerby, Thes. Conch. (*Tapes*), vol. ii., p. 695., pl. 150, f. 120.—Durban. The usual habitat of this species is the Mediterranean, but it does not appear to be common anywhere.

✓ CYPRICARDIA ANGULATA, *Lamarck*, Reeve, Conch. Icon., fig. 2.—Natal.

✓ CARDIUM TENUICOSTATUM, *Lamarck*, Reeve, Conch. Icon. *Cardium*, pl. 10, fig. 50.—Natal. Common in several localities on the Australian coast.

✓ CARDIUM RUGOSUM, *Lamarck*, Reeve, Conch. Icon. *Cardium*, pl. 14, fig. 68.—Natal. Widely distributed in the Indian Ocean, Australia, and South Sea.

✓ CARDIUM RUBICUNDUM, *Reeve*, Conch. Icon. *Cardium*, pl. 9, fig. 44.—Natal.

✓ CARDIUM PAPYRACEUM, *Chemnitz*, Reeve, Conch. Icon., pl. 2, fig. 9.—Natal. China Sea, Philippines, &c.

✓ CARDIUM TURTONI, *Sowerby*, pl. vii., fig. 4, Journal of Conchology, vol. 7, p. 14.—Port Elizabeth.

✓ CARDIUM BURNUPI, *Sowerby*, n. sp., pl. viii., f. 25. Testa subcircularis inflata, crassiuscula, straminea, carneo-fusco tincta radiatim costata ; costis 29 angustis, sub-remotis anticis fornicato squamatis, medianis serratis, posticis aculeatis.

Diam -antero-post 44, umbono-marg, 43 millim.

Hab. Durban.

This species (of which I have only seen odd valves) is intermediate in character between *C lima*, Gmelin, and *C. aculeatum*, Linn.

✓ CARDIUM ADAMSI, *Reeve*, Moll. Voy. Samarang, pl. 22, fig. 2

CHAMA IOSTOMA, *Conrad*, Reeve, Conch. Icon. (*Chama*), pl. 2, fig. 7.—Natal.

LUCINA EXASPERATA, *Reeve*, Conch. Icon. (*Lucina*), pl. 1, fig. 4.—Durban.

LUCINA (CODAKIA) PECTEN, *Lamarck*, Reeve, Conch. Icon., (*Lucina*) sp. 38.—St. John's, Durban.

LUCINA (DIVARICELLA) QUADRISULCATA, *D'Orbigny.*— *Lucina Eburnea*, Reeve, " Conch. Icon." (*Lucina*), pl. 8, sp. 49, —Natal. A species of wide distribution, Hong Kong, St. Helena, &c.

LORIPES CLAUSUS, *Philippi*, Abbild, und Beschr. Conch. vol. iii., Lucina pl. 2, fig. 2.—Natal. This is the shell quoted by me, p. 61, as *Loripes lacteus*. There are specimens in the British Museum from Mozambique.

SCINTILLA COMPTA, n. sp. (pl. 6, fig. 28). Testa oblongo-ovalis, compressiuscula, tenuis, æquivalvis, fere æquilateralis, alba, nitens ; margo dorsalis utrinque arcuatim declivis ; valvis utrinque paulo hiantibus, concentrice leviter et irregu-lariter rugatis ; umbones leviter prominentes, parviusculi. Antero-post. 12.50, umbono-marg. 8 millim.
Hab. Durban.

SCINTILLA QUEKETTI, n. sp. (pl. 8, figs. 20, 21). Testa sub-quadrato oblonga, æquilateralis, leviter inflata, alba, nitens, irregulariter concentrice rugata, clausa ; umbones vix prominentes, obtusiusculi ; margo dorsalis rectiusculus, later-ibus leviter rotundatis, margo ventralis levissime arcuatus, vel rectiusculus.
Antero-post 14, umbono-marg. 9.50.
Hab. Durban (Quekett).

SCINTILLA ELONGATA, n. sp. (pl. 8, fig. 24). Testa auguste oblonga, cylindracea, alba, tenuissima, leviter inæquilateralis, lateribus regulariter rotundatis ; umbones vix prominentes, paulo ante medium locati ; valvis vix hiantibus.
Antero-post 12, umbono-marg. 5.50 millim.
Hab. Durban (Burnup).
A very thin white shell, with valves scarcely gaping, distinguished by its narrow elongated form.

SCINTILLA DURBANENSIS, n. sp. (pl. 8, figs. 22, 23). Testa oblongo-ovalis, tenuis, alba, fere æquilateralis; umbones acuti, vix prominentes; margo dorsalis utrinque arcuatim paulo declivis ; hiatus ventralis angustus.

Antero-post 9, umbono—marg. 5 millim.
Hab., Durban (Burnup).
This shell is narrower than S. *Compta*, and has a rather narrow but decided ventral hiatus.

✓ SOLENOMYA TOGATA, *Poli* (= *Mediterranea*, Lamk), Reeve, Conch. Icon. (*Solemya*), fig. 2.—Durban.

✓ SEPTIFER NICOBARICUS, *Chemnitz*, Reeve, Conch. Icon. (*Mytilus*), pl. 9, fig. 42.—Durban.

✓ PINNA MADIDA, *Reeve*, Conch. Icon., pl. 17, fig. 31.— Durban.

. PINNA SACCATA, *Linn.*, Reeve, Conch. Icon., pl. 4, fig. 6.— Natal.

✓ PINNA SERRA, *Reeve*, Conch. Icon., pl. 23, f. 43.—Durban.

PINNA VEXILLUM, *Born*, Reeve, Conch. Icon., pl. 19, fig. 36.—Durban.

✓ PINNA SQUAMOSISSIMA, *Philippi*, Reeve, Conch. Icon., fig. 2 (as *P. seminuda*, Lam.)

. AVICULA (MELEAGRINA) FLABELLUM, *Reeve*, Conch. Icon. (*Avicula*), figs. 7. 8.—Durban. With this species I unite *A. imbricata., lacunata* and *muricata*, Reeve.

✓ AVICULA ZEBRA, *Reeve*, Conch. Icon., figs. 3, 6.—Port Elizabeth.

✓ MALLEUS TIGRINUS, *Reeve*, Conch. Icon. (*Malleus*), pl. 3, fig. 7.—Durban.

✓ MALLEUS LEGUMEN, *Reeve*, Conch. Icon., pl. 1, fig. 2.— Durban.

✓ PERNA ANOMIOIDES, *Reeve*, Conch. Icon. (*Perna*), pl. 3, fig. 11.—Durban.

✓ ARCA DIVARICATA, *Reeve*, Conch. Icon. (*Arca*), pl. 16, fig. 108.—Durban.

✓ ARCA (BARBATIA) CŒLATA, *Reeve*, Conch. Icon. (*Arca*), fig. 110.—Durban.

✓ PECTUNCULUS QUEKETTI, n. sp. (plate 7, figs. 8, 9).— Testa subquadrato rotundata, crassa, convexa, fusca, lineis numerosis albidis radiata, undique subtilissime radiatim striata; umbones centrales prominentes, acutiusculi, fere approximati; area elongata, angusta, sub-profunda; ligam-

entum crassiusculum ; cardo arcuatus, planulatus, latus ;
dentes 18, plus minusve elongati, rectiusculi ; pagina interna
alba ; impressiones musculares vivide rufo-fusco radiatim
tincti ; marginibus valde crenulatis.
    Antero-post. 65, umbono-marg. 65 m.m.
    Hab. Durban.
    This shell is quite distinct from the Mediterranean
species, and the vivid colouring of the muscular impressions
appears to be characteristic, although having only seen one
perfect specimen and two or three odd valves, I cannot with
certainty pronounce the character invariable.

    PECTEN SQUAMOSUS, *Gmelin*, Sow., Thes. Conch., vol. i.,
pl. 13, figs. 48, 50.—Natal.

    SPONDYLUS DUCALIS, *Chemnitz*, Sow., Thes. Conch., vol. i ,
pl. 85, fig. 16.—Natal.

    SPONDYLUS NICOBARICUS, *Chemnitz*, Sow., Thes. Conch.,
vol. i., pl. 88, fig. 48.—Natal.

    LIMA SQUAMOSA, *Lamarck*, Sow., Thes. Conch., vol. i., pl. 21,
fig. 1.—Natal. A species of very wide distribution from the
Mediterranean to Polynesia.

    LIMA HIANS, *Gmelin*, var. *tenera*, Turton (= *L. fragilis*,
Ch.), Reeve, Conch. Icon. (*Lima*), fig. 18.

    ANOMIA EPHIPPIUM, *Linn.*, Sow., Ill. Index of Brit. Shells,
pl. 8., fig. 18.—Durban.

    OSTREA LACERATA, *Hanley*, Proc. Zool. Soc. 1845, p. 106,
Conch. Icon., figs. 51 and 78, (as *O. lacerans* and *pes-tigris*)—
Limpopo R.

BRACHIOPODA.

    Agulhasia Davidsoni, *King*, Ann. and Mag. Nat. Hist ,
1871, vol. vii., p. 111, pl. xi., fig. 1.—Agulhas Bank.

ADDENDA.

(Received too late for figuring).

    APICALIA BIFORMIS, *Sowerby*, n. sp.—Testa ovato-
pyramidata, solidiuscula, polita, alba, anguste umbilicata,
antice globosa, postice acuminata ; spira elatiuscula, ad
apicem mucronata ; sutura angustissime canaliculata ;
anfractus 10, convexi, primi 5 contracti; ultimus rotundatus;
apertura latiuscula; labrum tenue, utrinque leviter sinuatum.

Hab. Durban.

An interesting species of which I have only seen one specimen. The first 5 whorls are narrowly contracted, from thence the spire suddenly widens, becoming regularly pyramidal, the body whorl being shortly rounded at the base. In form this shell resembles certain species of *Stylifer*, but its more opaque substance and smooth polished surface induce me to place it in the genus *Apicalia*, although I doubt whether the generic distinction is of much value. Unfortunately, I omitted to take the dimensions of this shell before returning it to S. Africa, but I think its length is about 12 or 13 m.m., or half an inch.

PANDORA SIMILIS, n. sp.—Testa oblonga, latiuscula, compressa, leviter inæquivalvis, valde inæquilateralis, concentrice irregulariter plicata, valva dextra subconcavo planulata, sinistra leviter convexa; umbones leviter prominentes, conjuncti; margo dorsalis anticus brevis declivis, posticus elongatus, incurvatus, duplicatus, vix rostratus; margo ventralis valde arcuatus.

Antero-post 16.50, umbono-marg. 10 millim.

Hab. Durban.

This species is broader than *P. inæquivalvis*, it closely resembles *P. rostrata*, Sow., but wants the posterior rostrum characteristic of that species.

SOLARIELLA SCULPTA, *Sowerby*, n. sp.—Testa depresse orbicularis, profunde umbilicata, supra fulvo-viridula, obscure fusco maculata, infra albida, fusco maculata; spira vix elevata; sutura planato depressa, plicata; anfractus 5, valde clathrati, convexi, superne angulati, spiraliter conspicue carinati, liris angustis numerosis obliquis clathrati; anfractus ultimus depresse rotundatus, infra convexus, costis spiralibus numerosis confertis instructus; umbilicus circularis, perspectivus, latiusculus, intus clathratus, extus crenulatus; apertura latiuscula, subcircularis, leviter obliqua, intus margaritacea; labrum tenue.

Diam. 4.50, alt. 2.25 millim.

Hab. Durban.

A depressed little shell, conspicuously latticed above the periphery, and closely lirate beneath. It has much the appearance of a small species of *Torinia*.

HAMINEA SUBCYLINDRICA, *Sowerby*, n. sp.—Testa oblonga, subcylindrica, tenuissima, alba, postice vix acuminata, leviter umbilicata, undique densissime transversim striata, striis

utrinque fortioribus; lateribus convexiusculis; apertura
mediocriter lata, postice producta, columella rectiuscula.

Hab. Durban.

Long. 8, lat. 4 millim.

A very fragile shell, very finely striated. In form it
somewhat resembles *H. brevis, (Quoy and Gaim.)*, but it is
rather more attenuated at the extremities, and consequently
less cylindrical.

NOTE.

Ziziphinus multiliratus, Sow. (P.Z.S., 1875, p. 127,
pl. 24, f. 10). is, I think, not S. African. The locality given
" Cape of Good Hope," being a mistake.

MARINE SHELLS OF SOUTH
AFRICA, 1892.

EMENDATIONS, 1897.

Page 4. For PYRULA read MELONGENA. The genus *Pyrula*,
Lam. belongs to the family *Doliidæ*, and is
restricted to the group of which *Bulla ficus*,
Linn. is the type.

Page 4. For METULA read TRITONIDEA, and add locality
Durban.

Page 6. For DEFRANCIA AMPLEXA read MANGILIA AMPLEXA.

Page 6. For DEFRANCIA CAPENSIS read CLATHURELLA
CAPENSIS.

Page 7. For DEFRANCIA read CLATHURELLA.

Page 7. Omit MANGILIA CLATHRATA. This was wrongly
identified, see CLATHURELLA VERRUCOSA, Sow.,
n. sp.

Page 7. MANGILIA COSTATA, add *var. coarctata*, Forbes.

Pages 7-9. For TRITON read LOTORIUM.[1] The well-known
generic name of *Triton* (Montfort) having been
previously used in another branch of Zoology,
it is unfortunately illegal to continue its use in
Malacology.

Page 9. RANELLA ARGUS, add locality Kalk Bay.

Page 9. RANELLA SEMIGRANOSA, R. CRUMENA, R. PUSILLA.
—Durban.

[1] LOTORIUM, Montfort, 1810.

Page 20.   Omit MARGINELLA EPIGRUS.   See M. BURNUPI, Sow., n. sp. .

Page 31.   CYPRÆA FIMBRIATA, add locality Durban.

Page 32.   CYPRÆA CITRINA, add locality Port Elizabeth.

Page 32.   CYPRÆA HELVOLA, C. CARNEOLA, C. CAURICA, C. MANRITIANA, and C Lamarcki.—Durban.

Page 33.   CYPRÆA UNDATA.—Durban.

Page 35.   CERITHUIM KOCHI, and C. MONILIFERUM.—Durban.

Page 40.   HIPPONYX AUSTRALIS.—Durban.

Page 44.   TROCHUS NIGROPUNCTATUS.—Durban.

Page 45.   CLANCULUS PUNICEUS. —Durban.

Page 50.   Omit CHITON MARGINATUS. The specimens referred to are C. ELIZABETHENSIS, Pilsbry.

Pages 50 and 51.   The POLYPLACOPHORA or *Chitons* are divided into the following sub-genera :—
DINOPLAX for *Chiton gigas*.
ACANTHOCHITES for *Chiton Garnoti*.
ISCHNOCHITON for *Chitons textilis, pruniosus, pertusus, tigrinus*, and *oniscus*.
CHÆTOPLEURA for *Chitons Watsoni*, and *pustulatus*.
CALLOCHITON for *Chiton castaneus*.
PLAXIPHORA for *Chiton Wahlbergi*.

Page 51.   Omit CHITON CAPENSIS (is *C. nigrovirens*).

Page 51.   „   CHITON MACGILLIVRAYI.

Page 51.   „   CHITON CARMICHÆLIS.

Page 51.   For CHITON NIGROVIRESCENS read C. NIGROVIRENS.

Page 55.   For MACTRA ADANSONI read M. GLABRATA, *Linn*, and place *M. Adansoni* in the synonymy. Add locality Durban.

Page 56.   LUTRARIA OBLONGA.—Natal.

Page 57.   TELLINA LITTORALIS.—Sub-genus MACOMA.

Page 58.   CYTHEREA (TIVELA) COMPRESSA.—Remove *C. polita* from synonymy.

Page 58.   Omit CYTHEREA (TIVELA) DOLADELLA as a species, and place it as synonym of C. POLITA, *Sowerby*.

Page 59.   MEROE OVALIS.—add loc., Durban.

Page 60.   Omit VENUS LAYARDI. The shells mistaken for this species are V. ARAKANA, *Nevill*.

Page 60.   PETRICOLA TYPICA.—Add loc., Durban.

Page 61.   LORIPES GLOBOSUS.—Add loc., Durban.

Page 65.   ARCA NIVEA.—Add loc. Durban.

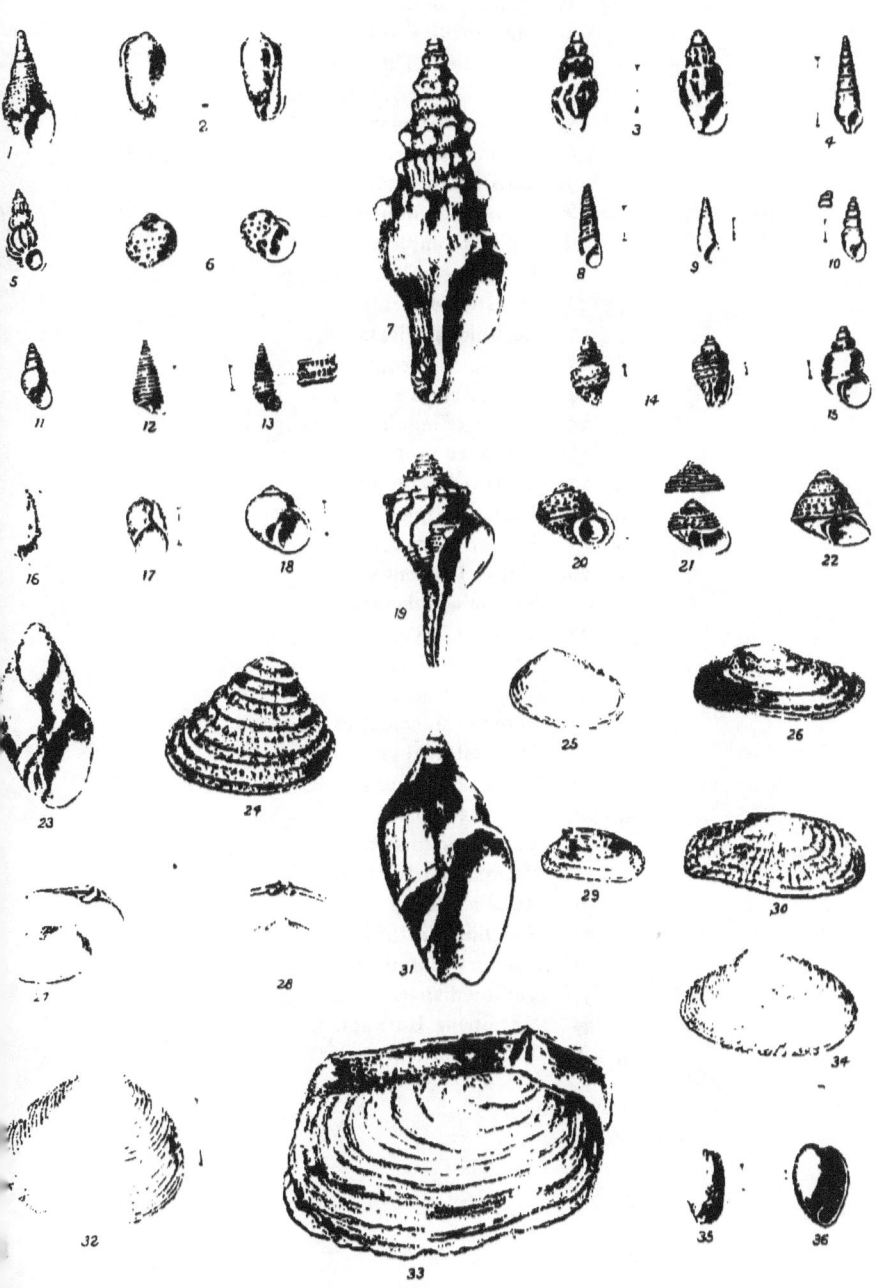

DESCRIPTION OF PLATE VI.

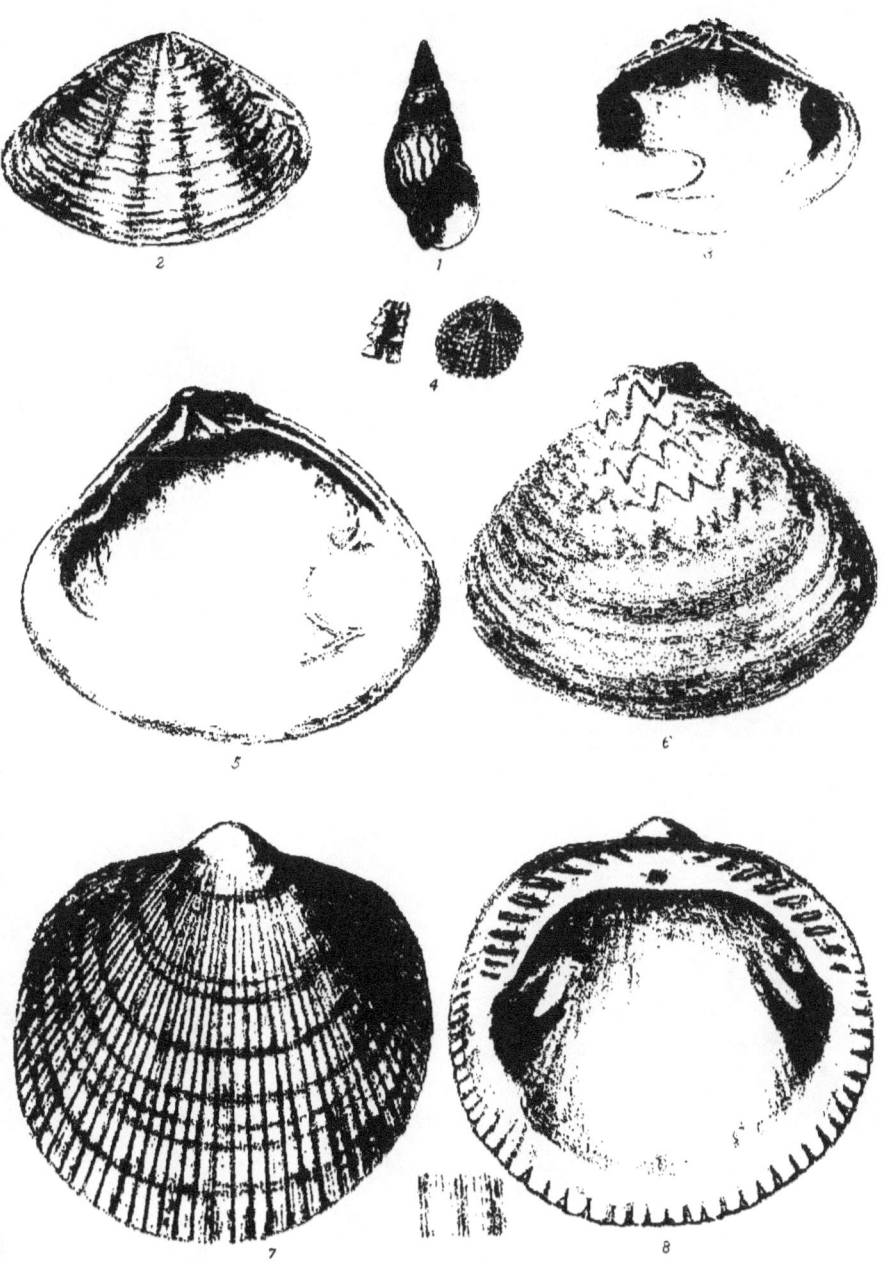

DESCRIPTION OF PLATE VII.

Fig. 1.   Bullia similis.
,, 2, 3.   Cytherea (Tivela) transversa.
,, 4.   Cardium Turtoni.
,, 5, 6.   Cytherea (Tivela) alucinans
,, 7, 8.   Pectunculus Queketti.

Plate VIII.

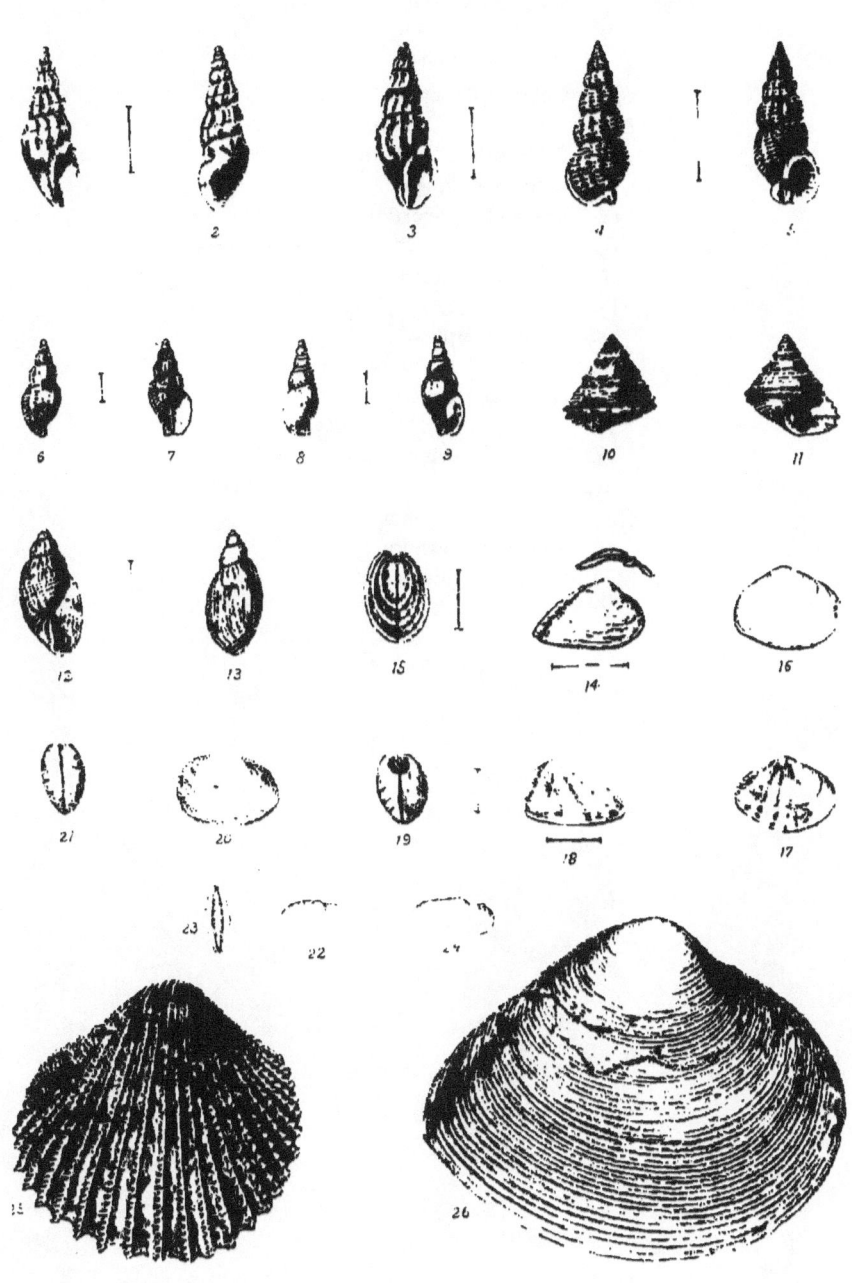

DESCRIPTION OF PLATE VIII.

INDEX TO GENERA.

—o—

www.ingramcontent.com/pod-product-compliance
Lightning Source LLC
Chambersburg PA
CBHW030908260626
47169CB00008B/2736